Library of Congress Cataloging-in-Publication Data
Chen, Chih-Yuan, 1975-
The best Christmas ever / written &
illustrated by Chih-Yuan Chen. -- 1st English ed. p. cm.
Summary: Little Bear's family is too poor to buy Chrismas presents,
but they get a surprise when they find some special gifts
that seem to have been left by "Toddler Chrismas."
[1. Bears--Fiction. 2. Chrismas--Fiction. 3. Toddlers--Fiction.
4. Bears--Fiction. 5. Christmas--Fiction. 6. Gifts--Fiction.] I. Title.
PZ7.C41817Bes 2005 [E]--dc22 2005013256
ISBN 0-9762056-2-9

To my dearest dad

The Best Christmas Ever

Chih-Yuan Chen

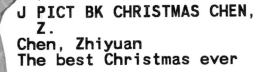

Heryin Books

Alhambra, California

The year had been tough
for Little Bear's father.
His business had failed
and he couldn't find work.
There was just enough money
left to feed the family.

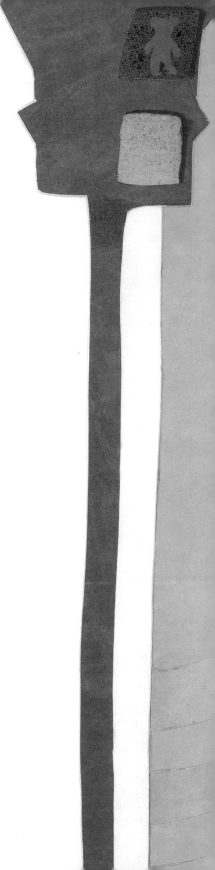

It was almost Christmas,
And everyone would be
expecting gifts–
What were they going to do?

Mother Bear counted their money
and said to Father Bear:
"We need to save this for the winter.
We can't afford presents for the
kids this year."

A few days before Christmas,
Mother Bear made Christmas decorations
with some old clothes that Little Bear
had outgrown. Little Bear's older sister
and brother decorated the windows,
hoping that Santa Claus would see.

That afternoon, Father Bear put on his
hat and went out to look for some tree
branches. He was going to make a
Christmas tree for the family.

Father Bear hung ornaments on the tree. He sprinkled the top with white flour, which sifted down to the branches below like fresh snow.

On Christmas Eve,
Mother cooked up a
delicious dinner with fish
that Father Bear had caught.

After dinner, everyone went
upstairs to bed. No one said much,
just a quiet "Good night."

Little Bear tossed and turned in his bed, unable to sleep. He called out to Farther Bear, asking to hear some Christmas stories.

When the stories were over, Little Bear said softly to his father: "Santa Claus brings us presents every year - he won't forget us this time."

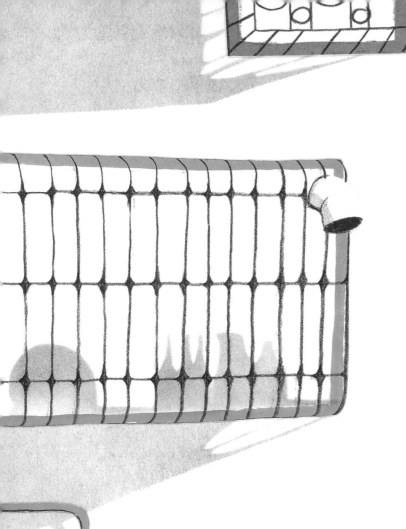

On Christmas morning, a gentle
ray of sunlight streamed through
the thin glass windows of the
Bears' house.

The ray illuminated five presents of different sizes, lying together under the Christmas tree.

Little Bear was the first one up. "Presents! Come and see, everyone!" he shouted, waking the whole family.

Each found a present bearing his or her name. Joyfully, Brother Bear exclaimed: "It had to be Santa Claus!"

Brother Bear opened his present.
"It's my kite!" he said in amazement.
"It got stuck in a tree and had this big
hole... But now it's as good as new!"

Sister Bear's present was an umbrella—
one she had left at the park, near the
swings. "Santa must have known how much I
wanted it back!" Sister Bear said excitedly.

Mother Bear's present
was a missing button from
her favorite dress.
She cupped the button in
her hand as though it
were a jewel.

Father Bear's present was the hat the wind
had blown off his head the day he collected
branches for the Christmas tree.
"How did Santa find my hat?" Father Bear
said with wonder.

Little Bear's present was his
favorite baseball glove, "It's
cleaned and shined up just like
brand-new!" he said.

Sister Bear discovered something strange:
under the tree were tiny footprints.
"Santa Claus must have made these when he came
with the presents... But why are they so small?"
she asked. Father Bear glanced at Little Bear
and said, "Maybe this Santa Claus is a dwarf,"
Mother Bear laughed and said, "If that's
the case, he's not 'Father' Christmas...
he's more like 'Toddler' Christmas!"

The whole of Christmas Day was spent discussing the mysterious gifts and, of course, the mysterious visit from "Toddler Christmas".

All those old familiar things,
newly presented, had rekindled
many fond memories.

And it was thus, that the Bears
had themselves...
the best Christmas ever.

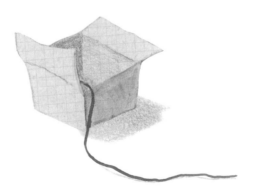

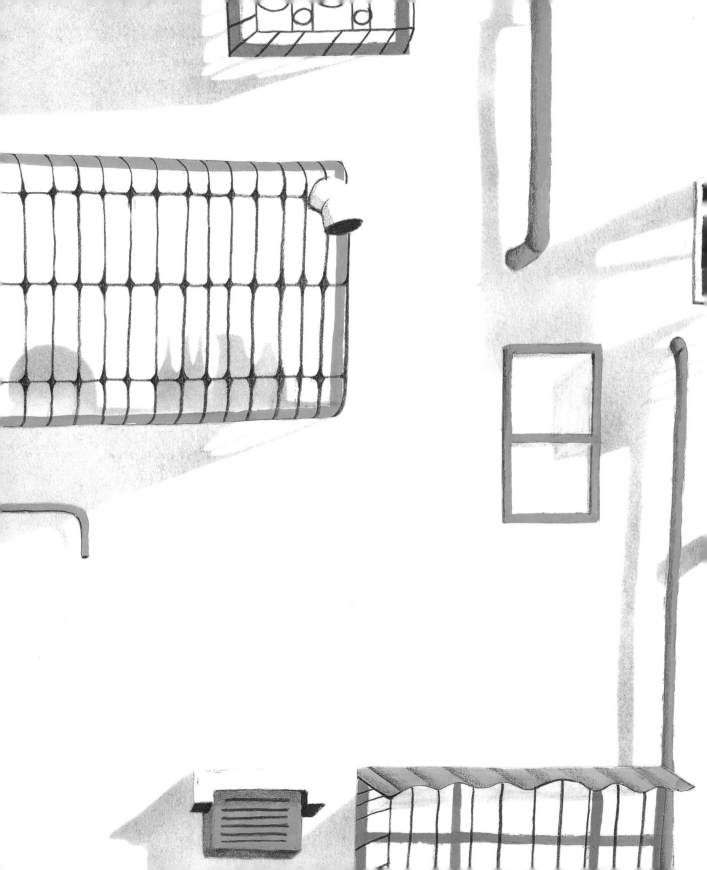